FAMILY STORIES

MR VIVEK KUMAR PANDEY SHAMBHUNATH

ISBN 979-888569644-9

Disclaimer : Disclaimer : During Writing This Book No character & No religious , No Relation Members Are Harmed. It's Only For Study & Entertainment Purpose. Do Not Take Seriously,Written By Mr Vivek Kumar Pandey.

Contents

Foreword

In This Book There Is Family Stories. A Story Tell By Her Father & Grandfather.During writing this book No character & No religious are harmed written by Mr Vivek Kumar Pandey. winner youngest writer award 1st rank in india 2020.He is only one writer can publish 830+ own book that was greatest successfull in his life.This All Credit Goes To My Super Hero Daddy.

Preface

Author biography in English :MY NAME IS VIVEK KUMAR PANDEY . I WAS BORN IN 30 SEP 2002,I AM FROM SURAT GUJARAT INDIA.MY DREAM WAS TO BE GOOD WRITERS ,MY FAMILY SUPPORTED ME TO SUCCESSFUL AND I CAN DO IT MY SELF.How do I write? That is a question, I believe, that can be honestly answered by me."CELEBRATING YOUNGEST WRITER AWARD WINNER IN GUJARAT 1ST RANK" MR PANDEY JI . I may think I did a good job writing something . The reader is the one who decides the quality of my writing. I do find writing to be natural to me and therefore find it to be a real challenge. My trick as a challenged writer is to do the best I can and know that I am happy with the final outcome. It may take a while to do my best and there may be quite a few problems I run into along the way.

I am not a greedy person those who are thinking about me and my self I never tried it anyone people suffering from sadness ,I trying to get promoted people suffering from happiness and joy in your Life Time. Now in current situation in India and also world people are unemployed and have no many but our indian governor help to people to get free food from ration card , i also take part in leadership team ,i am Motivational speaker , Film script writer. There was my two dream firstly writer and secondly actor & also my own film is upcoming soon i done almost completely completed script for my film .I AM GOING TO SAY WORD OF HEART TOUCH OUT PLEASE READ IT" , firstly i thanks my father he supports me in this field they always getting inspired me by own his words and behavior ,they always said that he was a biggest person in the world in future and also they purchase fruit and chocolate for me in anytime & anyway , firstly my father buy him then call me Vivek you want a chocolate i will say yes papa but how many tell me ,papa: you tell me how much i buy him i told 1 or 2 chocolate but my father purchase whole the boxes of chocolate and they get suprised me. MY FATHER WAS BORN IN " 20 SEPTEMBER" 1971 IN INDIA.

1) MY FATHER FAVORITE CLOTHES IS KURTA PAIJMA AND ALSO STYLES SHOE

2) FAVORITE SINGER IS KISHORE DA

3) FAVORITE STATE GUJARAT AND KOLKATA , HIS VILLAGE IN BIHAR

4) FAVORITE COLOR BLACK AND WHITE

THEY ALSO LOVE cricket like IPL and one day t-20 .they also like watching a News daily and heard the song daily ,they also interested in tik tok video but in current time tik tok is banned in india but also few videos are in you tube. In lockdown time my family and me very enjoy day daily. my father play daily ludo with his sister and son, daughter.they always loved tea and coffee anytime call me "I. I make it tea for my father but some reason after the April to june they are suffering from fever and cough , weakness on 6 June 2020 my father death. they not told me say bye bye his life. After death of 6 June on 10 june my mom and dad anniversary.but my father is Best in the world they can do anything for me please take care of father and respect it of your parents.

CHAPTER ONE

Ch : 1 Appreciation of Hard Work

- Ch : 1 Appreciation of Hard Work

One young academically excellent person went to apply for a managerial position in a big company. He passed the first interview, the director did the last interview, made the last decision. The director discovered from the CV that the youth's academic achievements were excellent all the way, from the secondary school until the postgraduate research, Never had a year when he did not score.

The director asked, "Did you obtain any scholarships in school?" The youth answered "none". The director asked, "Was it your father who paid for your school fees?" The youth answered, "My father passed away when I was one year old, it was my mother who paid for my school fees".

The director asked, "Where did your mother work?" The youth answered, "My mother worked as clothes cleaner. The director requested the youth to show his hands. The youth showed a pair of hands that were smooth and perfect".

The director asked, "Have you ever helped your mother wash the clothes before?" The youth answered, "Never, my mother always wanted me to study and read more books. Furthermore, my mother can wash clothes faster than me".

The director said, "I have a request. When you go back today, go and clean your mother's hands, and then see me tomorrow morning".

The youth felt that his chance of landing the job was high. When he went back, he happily requested his mother to let him clean her hands. His mother felt strange, happy but with mixed feelings, she showed her hands to the kid. The youth cleaned his mother's hands slowly. His tear fell as he did that. It was the first time he noticed that his mother's hands were so wrinkled, and there were so many bruises in her hands. Some bruises were so painful that his mother shivered when they were cleaned with water.

This was the first time the youth realized that it was this pair of hands that washed the clothes everyday to enable him to pay the school fee. The bruises in the mother's hands were the price that the mother had to pay for his graduation, academic excellence and his future. After finishing the cleaning of his mother's hands, the youth quietly washed all the remaining clothes for his mother. That night, mother and son talked for a very long time. Next morning, the youth went to the director's office.

The Director noticed the tears in the youth's eyes, asked: "Can you tell me what have you done and learned yesterday in your house?" The youth answered, "I cleaned my mother's hand, and also finished cleaning all the remaining clothes".

The Director asked, "please tell me your feelings". The youth said, "Number 1, I know now what is appreciation. Without my mother, there would not the successful me today. Number 2, By working together and helping my mother, only I now realize how difficult and tough it is to get something done. Number 3, I have come to appreciate the importance and value of family relationship".

The director said, "This is what I am looking for to be my manager. I want to recruit a person who can appreciate the help of others, a person who knows the sufferings of others to get things done, and a person who would not put money as his only goal in life. You are hired". Later on, this young person worked very hard, and received the respect of his subordinates. Every employee worked diligently and as a team. The company's performance improved tremendously.

- Moral: If one doesn't understand and experience the difficulty it takes to earn the comfort provided by their loved ones, than they will never value it.The most important thing is to experience the difficulty and learn to value hard work behind all the given comfort.

CHAPTER TWO

Ch : 2 A Soldiers Story

- Ch : 2 A Soldiers Story

A story is told about a soldier who was finally coming home after having fought in Vietnam. He called his parents from San Francisco. "Mom and Dad, I'm coming home, but I've a favor to ask. I have a friend I'd like to bring home with me. "Sure," they replied, "we'd love to meet him."

"There's something you should know," the son continued, "he was hurt pretty badly in the fighting. He stepped on a land mind and lost an arm and a leg. He has nowhere else to go, and I want him to come live with us."

"I'm sorry to hear that, son. Maybe we can help him find somewhere to live."

"No, Mom and Dad, I want him to live with us."

"Son," said the father, "you don't know what you're asking. Someone with such a handicap would be a terrible burden on us. We have our own lives to live, and we can't let something like this interfere with our lives. I think you should just come home and forget about this guy. He'll find a way to live on his own."

At that point, the son hung up the phone. The parents heard nothing more from him. A few days later, however, they received a call from the San Francisco police. Their son had died after falling from a building, they were told. The police believed it was suicide.

The grief-stricken parents flew to San Francisco and were taken to the city morgue to identify the body of their son. They recognized him, but to their horror they also discovered something they didn't know, their son had only one arm and one leg.

- Moral: The parents in this story are like many of us. We find it easy to love those who are good-looking or fun to have around, but we don't like people who inconvenience us or make us feel uncomfortable. We would rather stay away from people who aren't as healthy, beautiful, or smart as we are. Thankfully, there's someone who won't treat us that way. Someone who loves us with an unconditional love that welcomes us into the forever family, regardless of how messed up we are. Tonight, before you tuck yourself in for the night, say a little prayer that God will give you the strength you need to accept people as they are, and to help us all be more understanding of those who are different from us!.

CHAPTER THREE

Ch : 3 Evening Dinner with a Father

- Ch : 3 Evening Dinner with a Father

A son took his old father to a restaurant for an evening dinner. Father being very old and weak, while eating, dropped food on his shirt and trousers. Other diners watched him in disgust while his son was calm.

After he finished eating, his son who was not at all embarrassed, quietly took him to the wash room, wiped the food particles, removed the stains, combed his hair and fitted his spectacles firmly. When they came out, the entire restaurant was watching them in dead silence, not able to grasp how someone could embarrass themselves publicly like that. The son settled the bill and started walking out with his father.

At that time, an old man amongst the diners called out to the son and asked him, "Don't you think you have left something behind?".

The son replied, "No sir, I haven't".

The old man retorted, "Yes, you have! You left a lesson for every son and hope for every father".

The restaurant went silent.

- Moral: To care for those who once cared for us is one of the highest honors. We all know, how our parents cared for us for every little things. Love them, respect them, and care for them.

CHAPTER FOUR

Ch : 4 Father and Sons

- Ch : 4 Father and Sons

A father had a family of sons who were perpetually quarreling among themselves. When he failed to heal their disputes by his exhortations, he determined to give them a practical illustration of the evils of disunion.

One day he told his sons to bring him a bundle of sticks. When they had done so, he placed the fagot into the hands of each of them in succession, and ordered them to break it in pieces. They tried with all their strength, and were not able to do it. He next opened the fagot, took the sticks separately, one by one, and again put them into his sons' hands, upon which they broke them easily. He then addressed them in these words: "My sons, if you are of one mind, and unite to assist each other, you will be as strong as this fagot, uninjured by all the attempts of your enemies, but if you are divided among yourselves, you will be broken as easily as these sticks."

- Moral: Unity is strength.

CHAPTER FIVE

Ch : 5 Father Son Conversation

- Ch : 5 Father Son Conversation

Once day, father was doing some work and his son came and asked, "Daddy, may I ask you a question?" Father said, "Yeah sure, what it is?" So his son asked, "Dad, how much do you make an hour?" Father got bit upset and said, "That's none of your business. Why do you ask such a thing?" Son said, "I just want to know. Please tell me, how much do you make an hour?" So, father told him that "I make Rs. 500 per hour."

"Oh", the little boy replied, with his head down. Looking up, he said, "Dad, may I please borrow Rs. 300?" The father furiously said, "if the only reason you asked about my pay is so that you can borrow some money to buy a silly toy or other nonsense, then march yourself to your room and go to bed. Think why you are being so selfish. I work hard every day and do not like this childish behavior."

The little boy quietly went to his room and shut the door. The man sat down and started to get even angrier about the little boy's questions. How dare he ask such questions only to get some money? After about an hour or so, the man had calmed down, and started to think, "May be there was something he really needed to buy with that Rs. 300 and he really didn't ask for money very often!" The man went to the door of little boy's room and opened the door. "Are you a sleep, son?" He asked. "No daddy, I'm awake," replied the boy. "I've been thinking, maybe I was too hard on you earlier", said the man. "It's been a long day and I took out my aggravation on you, Here's the Rs.300 you asked for".

The little boy sat straight up, smiling "oh thank you dad!" He yelled. Then, reaching under his pillow he pulled some crippled up notes. The man, seeing that the boy already had money, started to get angry again. The little boy slowly counted out his money, then looked up at his father.

"Why do you want money if you already had some?" the father grumbled. "Because I didn't have enough, but now I do," the little boy replied. "Daddy I have Rs. 500 now. Can I buy an hour of your time? Please come home early tomorrow. I would like to have dinner with you". Father was dumbstruck.

• Moral: It's just a short reminder to all of you working so hard in life! We should not let time slip through our fingers without having spent some time with those who really matter to us, those close to our hearts. If we die tomorrow, the company that we are working for could easily replace us in a matter of days. But the family & friends we leave behind will feel the loss for the rest of their lives. And come to think of it, we pour ourselves more into work than to our family.

CHAPTER SIX

Ch : 6 Five More Minutes

- Ch : 6 Five More Minutes

While at the park one day, a woman sat down next to a man on a bench near a playground. "That's my son over there," she said, pointing to a little boy in a red sweater who was gliding down the slide. "He's a fine looking boy" the man said. "That's my daughter on the bike in the white dress."

Then, looking at his watch, he called to his daughter. "What do you say we go, Melissa?" Melissa pleaded, "Just five more minutes, Dad. Please? Just five more minutes." The man nodded and Melissa continued to ride her bike to her heart's content. Minutes passed and the father stood and called again to his daughter. "Time to go now?"

Again Melissa pleaded, "Five more minutes, Dad. Just five more minutes." The man smiled and said, "OK." "My, you certainly are a patient father," the woman responded.

The man smiled and then said, "Her older brother Tommy was killed by a drunk driver last year while he was riding his bike near here. I never spent much time with Tommy and now I'd give anything for just five more minutes with him. I've vowed not to make the same mistake with Melissa. She thinks she has five more minutes to ride her bike. The truth is, I get Five more minutes to watch her play."

- Moral: Life is all about making priorities, and family is one and only priority on top of all other, so spend all time you can with loved ones.

CHAPTER SEVEN

Ch : 7 Gift from Daughter

- Ch : 7 Gift from Daughter

The story goes that some time ago, a man punished his 3-year-old daughter for wasting a roll of gold wrapping paper. Money was tight and he became infuriated when the child tried to decorate a box to put under the Christmas tree. Nevertheless, the little girl brought the gift to her father the next morning and said, "This is for you, Daddy."

The man was embarrassed by his earlier overreaction, but his anger flared again when he found out the box was empty. He yelled at her, stating, "Don't you know, when you give someone a present, there is supposed to be something inside? The little girl looked up at him with tears in her eyes and cried, "Oh, Daddy, it's not empty at all. I blew kisses into the box. They're all for you, Daddy."

The father was crushed. He put his arms around his little girl, and he begged for her forgiveness.

Only a short time later, an accident took the life of the child. It is also told that her father kept that gold box by his bed for many years and, whenever he was discouraged, he would take out an imaginary kiss and remember the love of the child who had put it there.

- Moral: In a very real sense, each one of us, as humans beings, have been given a gold container filled with unconditional love from our children, family members, friends, and God. There is simply no other possession, anyone could hold, more precious than this.

CHAPTER EIGHT

Ch : 8 Grandpas Table

- Ch : 8 Grandpas Table

A frail old man went to live with his son, daughter-in- law, and four-year old grandson. The old man's hands trembled, his eyesight was blurred, and his step faltered. The family ate together at the table. But the elderly grandfather' s shaky hands and failing sight made eating difficult. Peas rolled off his spoon onto the floor. When he grasped, the glass, milk spilled on the tablecloth.

The son and daughter-in- law became irritated with the mess. "We must do something about Grandfather, " said the son. "I've had enough of his spilled milk, noisy eating, and food on the floor." So the husband and wife set a small table in the corner. There, Grandfather ate alone while the rest of the family enjoyed dinner. Since Grandfather had broken a dish or two, his food was served in a wooden bowl. When the family glanced in Grandfather' s direction, sometimes he had a tear in his eye as he sat alone. Still, the only words the couple had for him were sharp admonitions when he dropped a fork or spilled food. The four-year-old watched it all in silence.

One evening before supper, the father noticed his son playing with wood scraps on the floor. He asked the child sweetly, "What are you making?" Just as sweetly, the boy responded, "Oh, I am making a little bowl for you and Mama to eat your food in when I grow up." The four-year-old smiled and went back to work. The words so struck the parents that they were speechless. Then tears started to stream down their cheeks. Though no word was spoken, both knew what must be done.

That evening the husband took Grandfather' s hand and gently led him back to the family table. For the remainder of his days he ate every meal with the family. And for some reason, neither husband nor wife seemed to care any longer when a fork was dropped, milk spilled, or the tablecloth soiled.

- Moral: Children are remarkably perceptive. Their eyes ever observe, their ears ever listen, and their minds ever process the messages they absorb. If they see us patiently provide a happy home atmosphere for family members, they will imitate that attitude for the rest of their lives. The wise parent realizes that every day the building blocks are being laid for the child's future. Let's be wise builders and role models. Because Children are our future. Life is about people connecting with people, and making a positive difference. Take care of yourself, ... and those you love, ... today, ... and everyday!

CHAPTER NINE

Ch : 9 Making Relations Special

- Ch : 9 Making Relations Special

When I was a kid, my Mom liked to make breakfast food for dinner every now and then. And I remember one night in particular when she had made dinner after a long, hard day at work. On that evening so long ago, my Mom placed a plate of eggs, sausage and extremely burned biscuits in front of my dad. I remember waiting to see if anyone noticed! Yet all dad did was reached for his biscuit, smile at my Mom and ask me how my day was at school. I don't remember what I told him that night, but I do remember watching him smear butter and jelly on that biscuit and eat every bite!

When I got up from the table that evening, I remember hearing my Mom apologize to my dad for burning the biscuits. And I'll never forget what he said: "Honey, I love burned biscuits."

Later that night, I went to kiss Daddy good night and I asked him if he really liked his biscuits burned. He wrapped me in his arms and said, "Your Momma put in a hard day at work today and she's real tired. And besides – a little burned biscuit never hurt anyone!"

- Moral: Life is full of imperfect things and imperfect people. I'm not the best at hardly anything, and I forget birthdays and anniversaries just like everyone else. But what I've learned over the years is that learning to accept each others faults – and choosing to celebrate each others differences – is one of the most important keys to creating a healthy, growing, and lasting relationship.

Ch : 10 Mothers Sacrifice

- Ch : 10 Mothers Sacrifice

My mom only had one eye. I hated her... she was such an embarrassment. My mom ran a small shop at a flea market. She collected little weeds and such to sell... anything for the money we needed she was such an embarrassment. There was this one day during elementary school.

I remember that it was field day, and my mom came. I was so embarrassed. How could she do this to me? I threw her a hateful look and ran out. The next day at school... "Your mom only has one eye?!" and they taunted me.

I wished that my mom would just disappear from this world so I said to my mom, "Mom, why don't you have the other eye?! You're only going to make me a laughingstock. Why don't you just die?" My mom did not respond. I guess I felt a little bad, but at the same time, it felt good to think that I had said what I'd wanted to say all this time. Maybe it was because my mom hadn't punished me, but I didn't think that I had hurt her feelings very badly.

That night... I woke up, and went to the kitchen to get a glass of water. My mom was crying there, so quietly, as if she was afraid that she might wake me. I took a look at her, and then turned away. Because of the thing I had said to her earlier, there was something pinching at me in the corner of my heart. Even so, I hated my mother who was crying out of her one eye. So I told myself that I would grow up and become successful, because I hated my one-eyed mom and our desperate poverty.

Then I studied really hard. I left my mother and came to Seoul and studied, and got accepted in the Seoul University with all the confidence I had. Then, I got married. I bought a house of my own. Then I had kids, too.

Now I'm living happily as a successful man. I like it here because it's a place that doesn't remind me of my mom.

This happiness was getting bigger and bigger, when someone unexpected came to see me "What?! Who's this?!" It was my mother... Still with her one eye. It felt as if the whole sky was falling apart on me. My little girl ran away, scared of my mom's eye. And I asked her, "Who are you? I don't know you!!" as if I tried to make that real. I screamed at her "How dare you come to my house and scare my daughter! Get out of here now!!" And to this, my mother quietly answered, "oh, I'm so sorry. I may have gotten the wrong address," and she disappeared. Thank goodness... she doesn't recognize me. I was quite relieved. I told myself that I wasn't going to care, or think about this for the rest of my life.

Then a wave of relief came upon me... one day, a letter regarding a school reunion came to my house. I lied to my wife saying that I was going on a business trip. After the reunion, I went down to the old shack, that I used to call a house...just out of curiosity there, I found my mother fallen on the cold ground. But I did not shed a single tear. She had a piece of paper in her hand.... it was a letter to me.

She wrote:

My son, I think my life has been long enough now. And... I won't visit Seoul anymore... but would it be too much to ask if I wanted you to come visit me once in a while? I miss you so much. And I was so glad when I heard you were coming for the reunion. But I decided not to go to the school.... For you... I'm sorry that I only have one eye, and I was an embarrassment for you. You see, when you were very little, you got into an accident, and lost your eye. As a mother, I couldn't stand watching you having to grow up with only one eye... so I gave you mine... I was so proud of my son that was seeing a whole new world for me, in my place, with that eye. I was never upset at you for anything you did. The couple times that you were angry with me. I thought to myself, 'it's because he loves me.' I miss the times when you were still young around me. I miss you so much. I love you. You mean the world to me.

My World Shattered. I hated the person who only lived for me . I cried for My Mother, I didn't know of any way that will make up for my worst deeds...

- Moral: Never Ever hate anyone for their disabilities. Never disrespect your parents, don't ignore and under estimate their sacrifices. They give us life, they raise us better than they had been, they give and keep trying to give better than they ever had. They never wish unwell for their kids even in their wildest dreams. They always try showing right path and being motivator. Parents give up all for kids, forgive all mistakes made by kids. There is no way to repay what they done for kids, all we can do is try giving what they need and it is just time, love and respect.

CHAPTER ELEVEN

Ch : 11 Old Man and His Son

- Ch : 11 Old Man and His Son

An old man lived alone in Minnesota. He wanted to spade his potato garden, but it was very hard work. His only son, who would have helped him, was in prison. The old man wrote a letter to his son and mentioned his situation:

Dear Son, I am feeling pretty bad because it looks like I won't be able to plant my potato garden this year. I hate to miss doing the garden because your mother always loved planting time. I'm just getting too old to be digging up a garden plot. If you were here, all my troubles would be over. I know you would dig the plot for me, if you weren't in prison.

Love, Dad Shortly, the old man received this telegram: 'For Heaven's sake, Dad, don't dig up the garden!! That's where I buried the GUNS!!' At 4 a.m. the next morning, a dozen FBI agents and local police officers showed up and dug up the entire garden without finding any guns. Confused, the old man wrote another note to his son telling him what had happened, and asked him what to do next. His son's reply was: 'Go ahead and plant your potatoes, Dad. It's the best I could do for you, from here.'

- Moral: No Matter where you are in the World, If you have decided to do something deep from your heart, you can do it. It is the thought that matters, not where you are or where the person is.

CHAPTER TWELVE

Ch : 12 Rose for Mother

- Ch : 12 Rose for Mother

A man stopped at a flower shop to order some flowers to be wired to his mother who lived two hundred miles away. As he got out of his car he noticed a young girl sitting on the curb sobbing. He asked her what was wrong and she replied, "I wanted to buy a red rose for my mother. But I only have seventy-five cents, and a rose costs two dollars."

The man smiled and said, "Come on in with me. I'll buy you a rose." He bought the little girl her rose and ordered his own mother's flowers. As they were leaving he offered the girl a ride home. She said, "Yes, please! You can take me to my mother." She directed him to a cemetery, where she placed the rose on a freshly dug grave.

The man returned to the flower shop, canceled the wire order, picked up a bouquet and drove the two hundred miles to his mother's house.

- Moral: Life is Short. Spend much time as you can loving and caring people who love you. Enjoy each moment with them before it's too late. There is nothing important than family.

CHAPTER THIRTEEN

Ch : 13 The Boy and a Tree

- Ch : 13 The Boy and a Tree

A long time ago, there was a huge apple tree. A little boy loved to come andplay around it everyday. He climbed to the treetop, ate the apples, took a napunder the shadow.. he loved the tree and the tree loved to play with him. Timewent by.. the little boy had grown up and he no longer played around the treeevery day.

One day, the boy came back to the tree and he looked sad. 'Come and play withme' the tree asked the boy. 'I am no longer a kid, I do not play around treesany more' the boy replied. 'I want toys. I need money to buy them.' 'Sorry, butI do not have money.. but you can pick all my apples and sell them. So, you willhave money.' The boy was so excited. He grabbed all the apples on the tree andleft happily. The boy never came back after he picked the apples. The tree wassad.

One day, the boy who now turned into a man returned and the tree was excited'Come and play with me' the tree said. 'I do not have time to play. I have towork for my family. We need a house for shelter. Can you help me?" Sorry, but Ido not have any house. But you can chop off my branches to build your house.' Sothe man cut all the branches of the tree and left happily. The tree was glad tosee him happy but the man never came back since then. The tree was again lonelyand sad.

One hot summer day, the man returned and the tree was delighted. 'Come andplay with me!' the tree said. 'I am getting old. I want to go sailing to relaxmyself. Can you give me a boat?' said the man. 'Use my trunk to build your boat.You can sail far away and be happy.' So the man cut the tree trunk to make aboat. He went sailing and never showed up for a long time.

Finally, the man returned after many years. 'Sorry, my boy. But I do not haveanything for you anymore. No more apples for you' the tree said. 'No problem, Ido not have any teeth to bite' the man replied. 'No more trunk for you to climbon' the tree said. 'I am too old for that now' the man said. 'I really cannotgive you anything.. the only thing left is my dying roots' the tree said withtears. 'I do not need much now, just a place to rest. I am tired after all theseyears' the man replied. 'Good! Old tree roots are the best place to lean on andrest, Come, come sit down with me and rest.' The man sat down and the tree wasglad and smiled with tears..

- Moral: The tree is like our parents. When we were young, we loved to play with our Mum and Dad.. When we grow up, we leave them.. only come to them when we need something or when we are in trouble. No matter what, parents will always be there and give everything they could just to make you happy. You may think the boy is cruel to the tree, but that is how all of us treat our parents. We take them for granted we don't appreciate all they do for us until it's too late.

Ch : 14 The Giving Tree

- Ch : 14 The Giving Tree

Once upon a time, there lived a big mango tree. A little boy loved to come and play around it everyday. He climbed to the tree top, ate the mangoes, took a nap under the shadow... He loved the tree and the tree loved to play with him. Time went by, The little boy grew, and he no longer played around the tree.

One day, the boy came back to the tree with a sad look on his face. "Come and play with me," the tree asked the boy. "I am no longer a kid, I don't play around trees anymore." The boy replied, "I want toys. I need money to buy them." "Sorry, I don't have money... but you can pick all my mangoes and sell them so you will have money." The boy was so excited. He picked all the mangoes on the tree and left happily. The boy didn't come back. The tree was sad.

One day, the boy grown into a man returned. The tree was so excited. "Come and play with me," the tree said. "I don't have time to play. I have to work for my family. We need a house for shelter. Can you help me?" "Sorry, I don't have a house, but you can chop off my branches to build your house." So the man cut all the branches off the tree and left happily. The tree was glad to see him happy but the boy didn't come back afterward. The tree was again lonely and sad.

One hot summer day, the man returned and the tree was delighted. "Come and play with me!" The tree said. "I am sad and getting old. I want to go sailing to relax myself. Can you give me a boat?" "Use my trunk to build your boat. You can sail far away and be happy." So the man cut the tree trunk to make a boat. He went sailing and didn't come back for a long time.

Finally, the man returned after he had been gone for so many years. "Sorry, my boy, but I don't have anything for you anymore. No more mangoes to give you." The tree said. "I don't have teeth to bite," the man replied. "No more trunk for you to climb on." "I am too old for that now," the man said.

"I really can't give you anything, the only thing left is my dying roots," the tree said with sadness. "I don't need much now, just a place to rest. I am tired after all these years," the man replied. "Good! Old tree roots are the best place to lean on and rest. Come sit down with me and rest." The boy sat down and the tree was glad and smiled.

- Moral:The tree in the story represents our parents. When we areyoung, we love to play with them. When we growup, we leavethem and only come back when we need help. Parents sacrifice their lives for us. Never Forget their sacrifices. Give them Love and Care before its too late.

CHAPTER FIFTEEN

Ch : 15 The Praying Hands

- Ch : 15 The Praying Hands

Back in the fifteenth century, in a tiny village near Nuremberg, lived a family with eighteen children. Eighteen! In order merely to keep food on the table for this mob, the father and head of the household, a goldsmith by profession, worked almost eighteen hours a day at his trade and any other paying chore he could find in the neighborhood. Despite their seemingly hopeless condition, two of Albrecht Durer the Elder's children had a dream. They both wanted to pursue their talent for art, but they knew full well that their father would never be financially able to send either of them to Nuremberg to study at the Academy.

After many long discussions at night in their crowded bed, the two boys finally worked out a pact. They would toss a coin. The loser would go down into the nearby mines and, with his earnings, support his brother while he attended the academy. Then, when that brother who won the toss completed his studies, in four years, he would support the other brother at the academy, either with sales of his artwork or, if necessary, also by laboring in the mines.

They tossed a coin on a Sunday morning after church. Albrecht Durer won the toss and went off to Nuremberg. Albert went down into the dangerous mines and, for the next four years, financed his brother, whose work at the academy was almost an immediate sensation. Albrecht's etchings, his woodcuts, and his oils were far better than those of most of his professors, and by the time he graduated, he was beginning to earn considerable fees for his commissioned works.

When the young artist returned to his village, the Durer family held a festive dinner on their lawn to celebrate Albrecht's triumphant homecoming. After a long and memorable meal, punctuated with music and laughter, Albrecht rose from his honored position at the head of the table to drink a toast to his beloved brother for the years of sacrifice that had enabled Albrecht to fulfill his ambition. His closing words were, "And now, Albert, blessed brother of mine, now it is your turn. Now you can go to Nuremberg to pursue your dream, and I will take care of you."

All heads turned in eager expectation to the far end of the table where Albert sat, tears streaming down his pale face, shaking his lowered head from side to side while he sobbed and repeated, over and over, "No ...no ...no ...no."

Finally, Albert rose and wiped the tears from his cheeks. He glanced down the long table at the faces he loved, and then, holding his hands close to his right cheek, he said softly, "No, brother. I cannot go to Nuremberg. It is too late for me.

Look ... look what four years in the mines have done to my hands! The bones in every finger have been smashed at least once, and lately I have been suffering from arthritis so badly in my right hand that I cannot even hold a glass to return your toast, much less make delicate lines on parchment or canvas with a pen or a brush. No, brother ... for me it is too late."

More than 450 years have passed. By now, Albrecht Durer's hundreds of masterful portraits, pen and silver-point sketches, watercolors, charcoals, woodcuts, and copper engravings hang in every great museum in the world, but the odds are great that you, like most people, are familiar with only one of Albrecht Durer's works.

More than merely being familiar with it, you very well may have a reproduction hanging in your home or office.

One day, to pay homage to Albert for all that he had sacrificed, Albrecht Durer painstakingly drew his brother's abused hands with palms together and thin fingers stretched skyward. He called his powerful drawing simply "Hands," but the entire world almost immediately opened their hearts to his great masterpiece and renamed his tribute of love "The Praying Hands."

- Moral : The next time you see a copy of that touching creation, take a second look. Let it be your reminder, if you still need one, that no one – no one – ever makes it alone!

CHAPTER SIXTEEN

Ch : 16 The Ship of Friendship

- Ch : 16 The Ship of Friendship

A voyaging ship was wrecked during a storm at sea and only two of the men on it were able to swim to a small, desert like island.

The two survivors who have been a good friends, not knowing what else to do, agreed that they had no other recourse but to pray to God. However, to find out whose prayer was more powerful, they agreed to divide the territory between them and stay on opposite sides of the island.

The first thing they prayed for was food. The next morning, the first man saw a fruit-bearing tree on his side of the land, and he was able to eat its fruit. The other man's parcel of land remained barren.

After a week, the first man was lonely and he decided to pray for a wife. The next day, another ship was wrecked, and the only survivor was a woman who swam to his side of the land. On the other side of the island, there was nothing.

Soon the first man prayed for a house, clothes, more food. The next day, like magic, all of these were given to him. However, the second man still had nothing. Finally, the first man prayed for a ship, so that he and his wife could leave the island. In the morning, he found a ship docked at his side of the island. The first man boarded the ship with his wife and decided to leave the second man on the island.

He considered the other man unworthy to receive God's blessings, since none of his prayers had been answered.As the ship was about to leave, the first man heard a voice from heaven booming, "Why are you leaving your companion on the island?"

"My blessings are mine alone, since I was the one who prayed for them," the first man answered. "His prayers were all unanswered and so he does not deserve anything."

"You are mistaken!" the voice rebuked him. "He had only one prayer, which I answered. If not for that, you would not have received any of my blessings."

"Tell me," the first man asked the voice, "What did he pray for that I should owe him anything?"

"He prayed that all your prayers be answered "

• Moral: For all we know, our blessings are not the fruits of our prayers alone, but those of another praying for us (Congregational Prayer). Value your friends, don't leave your loved ones behind.

CHAPTER SEVENTEEN

Ch : 17 The White Elephant

- Ch : 17 The White Elephant

Once upon a time, there lived a herd of eighty thousand elephants at the bottom of the majestic Himalayas. Their leader was a magnificent and rare white elephant who was an extremely kind-hearten soul. He greatly loved his mother who had grown blind and feeble and could not look out for herself.

Each day this white elephant would go deep into the forest in search of food. He would look for the best of wild fruit to send to his mother. But alas, his mother never received any. This was because his messengers would always eat them up themselves. Each night, when he returned home he would be surprised to hear that his mother had been starving all day. He was absolutely disgusted with his herd.

Then one day, he decided to leave them all behind and disappeared in the middle of the night along with his dear mother. He took her to Mount Candorana to live in a cave beside a beautiful lake that was covered by gorgeous pink lotuses.

It so happened that one day, when the white elephant was feeding he heard loud cries. A forester from Benaras had lost his way in the forest and was absolutely terrified. He had come to the area to visit relatives and could not find his way out.

On seeing this big white elephant he was even more terrified and ran as fast as he could. The elephant followed him and told him not to be afraid, as all he wanted to do was to help him. He asked the forester why he was crying so bitterly. The forester replied that he was crying because he had been roaming the forest for the past seven days and could not find his way out.

The elephant told him not to worry as he knew every inch of this forest and could take him to safety. He then lifted him on to his back and carried him to the edge of the forest from where the forester went on his merry way back to Benaras.

On reaching the city, he heard that King Brahmadutta's personal elephant had just died and the King was looking for a new elephant. His heralds were roaming the city, announcing that any man who had seen or heard of an elephant fit for a King should come forward with the information.

The forester was very excited and immediately went up to the King and told him about the white elephant that he had seen on Mount Candorana. He told him that he had marked the way and would require the help of the elephant trainers in order to catch this fantastic elephant.

The King was quite pleased with the information and immediately dispatched a number of soldiers and elephant trainers along with the forester. After travelling for many days, the group reached the lake besides which the elephants resided.

They slowly moved down to the edge of the lake and hid behind the bushes. The white elephant was collecting lotus shoots for his mother's meal and could sense the presence of humans. When he looked up, he spotted the forester and realized that it was he who had led the King's men to him. He was very upset at the ingratitude but decided that if he put up a struggle many of the men would be killed. And he was just too kind to hurt anyone. So he decided to go along with them to Benaras and then request the benevolent King to be set free.

That night when the white elephant did not return home, his mother was very worried. She had heard all the commotion outside and had guessed that the King's men had taken away her son. She was scared that the King would ride him in to battle and her son would definitely be killed. She was also worried that there would be no one to look after her or even feed her, as she could not see. She just lay down and cried bitterly.

Meanwhile her son was led in to the beautiful city of Benaras where he was given a grand reception. The whole city was decorated and his own stable was gaily painted and covered with garlands of fragrant flowers. The trainers laid out a feast for their new state elephant who refused to touch a morsel. He did not respond to any kind of stimuli, be it the fragrant flowers or the beautiful and comfortable stable. He just sat there looking completely despondent.

The worried trainers went straight to report the situation to their King, as they were scared that the elephant would just waste away without any food or water. The King was extremely concerned when he heard what they had to say and went to the stable himself. He offered the elephant food from the royal table and asked him why he grieved in this manner. He thought that the elephant should be proud and honored that he was chosen as the state elephant and would get the opportunity to serve his King.

But the white elephant replied that he would not eat a thing until he met his mother. So the King asked him where his mother was. The elephant replied that she was back home on Mount Candorana and must be worried and hungry as she was blind and had no one to feed her and take care of her. He was afraid that she would die.

The compassionate King was touched by the elephant's story and asked him to return to his blind, old mother and take care of her as he had been doing all along. He set him free in love and kindness. The happy elephant went running home as fast as he could. And he was relieved to find that his mother was still alive. He filled his trunk with water and poured it over his sick mother who thought that it was raining. Then she cried out as she thought that some evil spirit had come to harm her and wished and prayed that her son was there to save her.

The white elephant gently bent over his blind mother and stroked her lovingly. She immediately recognized his touch and was overjoyed. Her son lifted her up and told her that the kind and compassionate King of Benaras had set him free and he was here to love and look after his mother forever.

His mother was absolutely thrilled and blessed the kind King with peace, prosperity and joy till the end of his days. She was so thankful to him for sending her son back home. The white elephant was able to take good care of his mother till the day she died. And when he died himself, the King erected a statue of him by the side of the lake and held an annual elephant festival there in memory of such a caring and noble soul.

- Moral: Always give affection and care to our dear ones. Always respect other's feelings.

CHAPTER EIGHTEEN

Ch : 18 The Wooden Bowl

- Ch : 18 The Wooden Bowl

A frail old man went to live with his son, daughter-in-law, and four-year old grandson. The old man's hands trembled, his eyesight was blurred, and his step faltered. The family ate together at the table. But the elderly grandfather's shaky hands and failing sight made eating difficult. Peas rolled off his spoon onto the floor. When he grasped the glass, milk spilled on the tablecloth.

The son and daughter-in-law became irritated with the mess. "We must do something about father," said the son. "I've had enough of his spilled milk, noisy eating, and food on the floor." So the husband and wife set a small table in the corner. There, Grandfather ate alone while the rest of the family enjoyed dinner. Since Grandfather had broken a dish or two, his food was served in a wooden bowl! When the family glanced in Grandfather's direction, sometime he had a tear in his eye as he sat alone. Still, the only words the couple had for him were sharp admonitions when he dropped a fork or spilled food.

The four-year-old watched it all in silence.

One evening before supper, the father noticed his son playing with wood scraps on the floor. He asked the child sweetly, "What are you making?" Just as sweetly, the boy responded, "Oh, I am making a little bowl for you and Mama to eat your food in when I grow up." The four-year-old smiled and went back to work . The words so struck the parents so that they were speechless. Then tears started to stream down their cheeks. Though no word was spoken, both knew what must be done.

That evening the husband took Grandfather's hand and gently led him back to the family table. For the remainder of his days he ate every meal with the family. And for some reason, neither husband nor wife seemed to care any longer when a fork was dropped, milk spilled, or the tablecloth soiled.

- Moral: You reap what you sow. Regardless of your relationship with your parents, you'll miss them when they're gone from your life. Always Respect, Care for and Love them.

Thank You So Much Message

For Your Supported & For Your Loves Thank You So Much. Have A Greatest Day Of Your. If I am successful today, because of my father, if he lived today, he would have been very happy, he will always and always be with me.